JOURNEY TO PEACE

Journey To Peace
Copyright © Blue Leaf Publishing LLC

All rights reserved. Published by Blue Leaf
Publishing LLC., Publishers since 2022.

No part of this publication may be reproduced, stored in a
means, electronic, mechanical, photocopying, recording, or
otherwise, without written permission of the publisher.
For information regarding permissions,
Write to Blue Leaf Publishing LLC.,
Attention: Permissions Department,
Blueleafpublishing1@gmail.com

10 9 8 7 6 5 4 3 2 1   11 12 13 14 15

Book design by Blue Leaf Publishing LLC
First edition, 2023
Printed in USA

Paperback ISBN: 979-8-218-13819-6
eBook ISBN: 979-8-9877128-0-1

JOURNEY TO PEACE

NAKIA KENYON

Preface

On Juneteenth 2020 Georgia experienced a great deal of involvement with the Black Lives Matter movement. Several protests were conducted throughout the day and days after the holiday had passed. After the death of George Floyd and Rayshard Brooks the streets were teaming with protests to show the national outrage over the death of African American men at the hands of police officers. There was also conflict in the Christian community over whether Christians should participate in the protest since violence was a possibility if the crowd became unruly. Some Christians conducted their own protests to promote social equality and some participated in community protests even though some of the things said there was against their beliefs.

The story is based on true events that happened to me as I researched the protests in Georgia. I participated in several protests and conversated with many people who were at the protests for different reasons. I wanted to write a story that expressed the varying opinions of the people I encountered at the protests. *Journey To Peace* has some aspects of my personal experiences with racism as well. This was a good way to round out the main character of the story. So, while you're reading know that not everything in the story is made up.

For my children: Kyron, Jacob, and Noah.
Never stop working toward your dreams.

CHAPTER ONE

The sun rises on another day without a job. I graduated from college, but the job market is tough and no one will give me an interview. I don't know what I would do without my parents' help right now. It's Friday morning, and I wake to see yet another news report of a black man dying at the hands of police. I can't believe this is happening again. I'm so sick of seeing this on the news, it's all anybody talks about. I want to scream and cry, 'God, why is this happening all the time? Why does everyone hate us?' Tears start to roll down my eyes, not because I'm sad, but because I'm so angry. What can I do with all this anger? I don't want to hurt anyone, but I just don't know what to do. Tears streaming down my face, I hear the news talk about protests that have started because of the wrongful deaths of black Americans. I'm not surprised people are starting to rise up and march together. The news says whole neighborhoods are protesting.

"That's amazing!" My face lights up as the tears quickly stop falling from my face. That's what I can do, I can join the protests! I can stand with other people just as angry as I am and show those police officers there are more of us than there are of them. I know protests like this have happened before, but I have to do something. I can't just sit here and hope it gets better; I have to take action. Action that is seen and heard by the people of this country. I've never protested anything before and I start guessing what I'm supposed to do now. What am I supposed to wear? How am I supposed to act? Everything is new, and it's making me nervous.

How do I find a protest to go to? With a determined look on my face, I try searching the internet for a protest I can go to and

I find more than I can count. Tomorrow is Juneteenth, so there are dozens of protests going on. There are several in Georgia, some are back-to-back. I believe I will go to the protest in Atlanta, Georgia. This protest is at Olympic Park, and it's supposed to be a big one.

"That's perfect!" I say victoriously. I'll be surrounded by people just as outraged as I am. I'm so angry and hurt. I need to be with people who think as I do. I know there has to be many people who want the killing to stop. Maybe a riot will break out, and we'll turn some cop cars over. That'll show them we'll fight back together and prove we are united in arms.

The protest is tomorrow morning, so I have to get ready now. Atlanta, Georgia is three and a half hours away from where I live in Tennessee, so I'll have to leave at around 4:30 in the morning to get there on time. I've never been to Olympic Park before, and I'm starting to get really excited. I can't wait to get involved in this movement. My life up to now has been all about me. I'm ready to be a part of something bigger, and now I have an opportunity to get involved with a movement that will inspire real change in the world.

The scene on the news has changed, and although I can see the sun is going to be shining tomorrow, I'm not interested in the weather right now. I have high hopes for this journey, and I know my life is about to change for the better. I'm not scared, though; I'm excited. I'm ready to play my part in making black lives matter.

CHAPTER TWO

Without a second thought, I run to my closet to look for a suitable backpack to take with me to the protest. My thoughts racing, I start making a rundown of what I'll need in my mind. It's the beginning of the summer months, so I'm going to need lots of water and maybe a small umbrella to shield me from the heat. Suddenly, I pause my search. A feeling of caution moves through my body and then alarm. I realize I'm about to surround myself with a mass of strangers, something to be avoided these days with COVID-19 infecting people around the world.

"Crap, I didn't think about that!" But I can't worry about that now, my sisters and brothers are dying every day. I have to act now and prove to myself I can make a difference in this world. I'll be safe and pack my mask. I know how to social distance, so I'll do that too. I can't help how emotional I feel. The tears come again, and I fall to my knees in the closet. "This will work. I will *make* it work. I know I'm only one person, but I won't be alone at the protest. I will have like-minded people by my side to support me and I will support them. That's how it works at these demonstrations. Before you know it, we'll have a community of protesters." The thought of having other people by my side makes my heart feel light, and I don't want to cry anymore. Pulling myself together, I resume looking for a bag. Finally, with delight, I find it. I reach down and pick up my old backpack from high school.

"I really need to learn to throw stuff away," I say as I hold the bag up, inspecting it for damage. It's in perfect shape. This will work just fine. The bag is light blue with white polka dots. "Not exactly Black Lives Matter looking," I say as I hold up the bag, but it will do in a pinch. The point is to be there and speak out. I'll shout louder than anyone else. That will make up for my brightly colored backpack.

I can still hear the news in the living room. A feeling of determination fills my body and I know that once my journey begins, there is no turning back. I will make a difference for the African American race and let those police know they cannot push us around. I firmly grip my backpack and begin filling it with things I might need for the trip. With energy to spare, I go through my list.

"Let's see. I need water, since it's blazing hot in Atlanta." Grabbing hand sanitizer, I'm reminded of the dangers of COVID. We might hold hands as we march down the street, so I need to be prepared for that. I'll bring a mask too, so I can still talk to people. Maybe I should bring some snacks with me. I don't know how long I'm going to be out there, so I should be prepared for the unexpected. I can't wait to get going! Tomorrow cannot come soon enough!

I'm usually a peaceful person, always smiling, but I don't feel like smiling right now. Right now, I want to scream! I have so much anger built up inside me, I could explode. I'm afraid to look in a mirror, because I might literally see smoke coming out of my ears. All black people have gone through some kind of discrimination in their lives. It doesn't matter if we have money or not. It doesn't matter where we live. We're never seen as equals in this world! Why, God? Why do our lives have to be this way? Well, I guess I'll find my answers on this trip. When I get to the protest, I'm going to let all my anger and frustration loose on the police and anyone there who might stand up for them. It feels good to know this is my path and I'm going to walk it with true conviction.

Since I'll only be in Georgia for a day, packing my bag doesn't take long. I look up Olympic Park on my phone and the surrounding areas. "Atlanta is pretty big and there are a lot of neighborhoods around where the protests are going to be at." Maybe they'll all band together and come to the protest as a community. Okay, that's a little unlikely, but it would still be really cool. Besides, there are too many protests for that to happen, but maybe because there are so many, some people might protest hop. I might do the same, since the one I'm going to is starting so early in the morning. That way I can protest all day instead of just protesting in the morning and then coming home. I'm not going to bother with mapping out my day. I'll just play it by ear, since I don't know when the first protest is going to end. Maybe it'll last into the night, since that's when I'm expecting the real demonstration to start. Maybe I should bring some snacks with me. I quickly find some peanut butter crackers and fruit snacks and put them in my backpack; that will do if I get hungry while I'm marching.

As the day goes by, I become more and more excited. Tomorrow is going to be life changing, I just know it. I wonder what other protests have happened in the past. What was that one my mom told me about? Oh yeah, Bloody Sunday. Information on that should be online. I grab my phone and do a search for Bloody Sunday. It doesn't take long for the information to pop up, but apparently Bloody Sunday is something that happened in Ireland. So, I try Bloody Sunday Alabama and I'm able to see the information I want. Wow, the marches in Selma were all about black people wanting to vote? So many people got hurt over something so simple. I vote, but it never occurred to me that the right to vote was something I needed to be thankful for. I have a lot of friends who don't bother with voting. After the protest is over, I think I'm going to give them a call and talk about voting. Change can come if everyone gets involved in their own way. If they don't want to protest, they can at least vote. We can show our ancestors their sacrifice wasn't for nothing. I look at some of the photos online. I see Caucasians standing with the black people as they march. I wonder what their reason for being there was. They got hurt, too. I wonder how their families felt about them being there. I can only guess as to their reasons, but I do believe it will take all of us to bring real change.

I decide to go to bed early so I can be well rested for the drive to Atlanta. I lay my head on my pillow and think about everything I want to accomplish with this trip. Maybe I'm being too optimistic with my expectations. I can't hope to accomplish equal rights for African Americans in one day. I know better than that, but I do believe I can do my part for positive change. As I close my eyes, I say a little prayer. "Dear Lord, please allow me to reach my destination without incident, and give me the courage to stand up for what's right. Thank you. In your glorious name, Jesus. Amen."

CHAPTER THREE

I was so excited last night I could hardly sleep at all. I kept thinking about the people I would meet or the things I would say. Before I realized it, the alarm went off.

"Wow, 4 o'clock already? Well, I guess it's time to get up and get going." I hurry to get dressed, grab a cup of coffee, get my bag, and head out the door. I decided to wear shorts, for obvious reasons, with a short-sleeve shirt and sneakers. I'll try to stay cool while marching, but that might be a challenge today. With sleepy eyes, I get in my car and make my way to Georgia.

The drive to Georgia is on a road familiar to me. My mother used to take me and my sisters to Georgia to visit family and her friends all throughout my childhood. So, being on the road now is more nostalgic than anything else. I remember long rides with sing-a-longs in the back seat with me and my sisters, headed toward destinations filled with pool parties and good, homecooked food. I remember trips to the city with my cousins where we laughed and gave some boys trying to talk to us fake names. I picked something simple like Kim, but my sister said her name was Andromeda. Of course, the guys knew our names were fake after hearing that! But it was okay, we all had a good laugh, even the guys.

Driving down the road, I can't help for smile at such a wonderful memory. Maybe I should have asked my sisters to come with me… On second thought, maybe not. I only had a day to get ready and they wouldn't have been able to get themselves together in time. Besides, this is something I feel really passionate about. I want to do this to prove something to myself. I want to prove I can be a part of something bigger than myself and make a difference. I'll invite them to the next protest. I'm sure there will be more than the ones happening today, and in more places than Georgia.

Minutes turn to hours and before long, I'm passing the *Welcome to Georgia* sign. This is awesome; I'm getting really excited about the protest. I'm going to scream at every officer I see! I'm going to make them see me and hear me. They're all haters… Why do they hate us so much?

As tears start to well in my eyes, I remember a time in high school when I was standing outside waiting for a friend. He was late and not at our usual spot, so I thought I would wait for him at the back of the school. This officer approached me and said, 'Hey, you can't be over here, it's for the buses.' I tried to explain to him I couldn't find my friend, and I was looking to see if he was there, when the officer just started yelling at me. He said he didn't care why I was there, and yelled at me to 'just move!' I was so scared, I almost cried right there. As I slowly walked away, I heard him tell a teacher, 'That's just how you have to talk to them.' Is that what I am? A *them*? Stop, I'm not going to cry anymore! It's time to make the officers cry! I'm not a 'them,' I'm a person with feelings and I'm going to make sure they know exactly how I feel!

The drive through the mountains goes slowly. There are big rigs everywhere, so they slow all the other cars down. "At this rate, I'm going to be late for the demonstration." The rig in front of me speeds up a little, and I take the opportunity to go around him. Cool, now I can speed up a little and get out of these mountains.

The sunshine is in my face, the radio plays songs I can dance to, and I'm feeling really good as the cityscape begins to show itself in the distance. Excitement builds up in my body as I come nearer and nearer to the city. It's about time. I can't wait to get there and see this protest for myself. Change starts today with this one act of freedom.

CHAPTER FOUR

I turn on my GPS and input the address for Olympic Park in Atlanta. Now I can navigate my way through the city, somewhere I've never been to alone before, and find the park. As I approach the city, I notice something. It's close to 8 a.m., but where is everyone? The streets are empty and there is trash all over the ground. Some buildings have their windows boarded up, and it doesn't look like any shops are open.

Look at this place. It looks like a ghost town around here. What happened? I wonder to myself as I drive through the streets. Then I remembered something from the news report.

The reporter said a riot broke out after the news of the police killing an unarmed black man got out. Shops were destroyed and people were running in the streets, looting as they went. I guess the store owners boarded everything up to stop their stores from being looted. But those people were angry and out of control. That's not what I want to do. I'm aiming my anger at the police, not the stores, so I'm not like *those* people. I have a clear goal in mind. Even if others get out of control, that doesn't mean I have to.

It isn't long before I turn a corner and see the six Olympic rings at the entrance of the park. "Finally, I made it! Oh no, the protest has already started!" I'll find a place to park quickly. "I don't see them marching yet, so I'm not too late to join in," I say nervously. Parking isn't easy, there are cars everywhere. I see some people coming out of a garage on a side street, but I see it too late and pass it. Navigating the roads in a city as big as Atlanta is not easy when you don't know where you're going, but

I'm able to park in an open lot not too far from the park.

I get out of my car and look around and notice swarms of people going to the park. Some had signs that said *Black Lives Matter*, and some said *No Justice, No Peace*, but everyone has a mask on, so I quickly grab mine and put it on. I feel a little unprepared since I don't have a sign, but I fall in line with everyone else making their way to the park. I stop at a crosswalk and look at the people standing next to me. I've never had a problem talking to new people, so I build up my courage and say hello to a man standing next to me.

"Hello, are you from Atlanta?"

"Yes, I am."

"I'm from Tennessee. This is my first protest."

The man smiled through his mask. "Well, that's great! I hope people come from all over."

We cross the street and he and the people with him continue toward the gate. I follow, but at a much slower pace. I can't help but look around and take all this in. It's shocking; the crowd is massive. There are people gathering around, forming a giant circle surrounding the outside of the park fence. The crowd inside the park is covering the grounds, so all I can see is people holding signs from one end of the park to the other. It's amazing to see so many people are here to fight for social change. But wait a minute, all these people are not black! There, mixed in with the black protesters, is a large number of white people. This protest is for the unlawful killing of a black man at the hands of white police officers. What are white people doing here? I guess it's reasonable to believe white people are upset over what happened, but why are they protesting?

I don't understand what's going on. Where are the mega phones? Why are people not shouting and pumping each other up to engage the police? As I look around the park, I notice a lot of children standing with their parents. "What are children doing here?" I say to myself. Their T-shirts say *Black Lives Matter*, but everyone is talking and listening to someone speak inside the park. It sounds a lot like a sermon. He's telling the crowd to pray for each other and the community. This isn't what I expected. Am I really in the right place?

I begin walking the perimeter of the park, going in a southerly direction to see if I can find a way in. There are people standing and watching from outside the gate. Others are selling Black Lives Matter T-shirts, hats and scarfs. They also have masks for sale too. I didn't think stuff like this would be going on. Inside the park, I can see people sitting and standing in front of a massive stage. Some Christian music is playing and people are singing along, while others are content with just listening. It's nice to see families participating in the protest together. Maybe if new generations get involved, protests won't be needed in the future.

This is great and all, but what happened to the scene I was expecting? Everyone is smiling and holding hands. This can't be right! Okay, I'm going to take a deep breath and think this through. The protest did just start, and I'm new to this. Maybe this is the information and reflection part of the protest. I'm sure as the protest goes on, it will become more of what I was hoping for. Not too aggressive, but not for children either. Yeah, that's it. I need to wait this out and everything will be fine. But I don't want to wait this out on the sidewalk around the park. I think I see a spot I can sit down inside the park by a tree. I'll go there and listen to the speaker. What he's saying isn't bad and could help keep the later demonstration from going too far. Okay, it's settled. I'll wait it out and express myself later.

CHAPTER FIVE

I walk to the front of the park, where a large crowd has gathered. It's hard to maneuver to the gate, but I finally make it there. I try to move closer into the park, when I'm stopped by a white woman at the entrance.

"You can't go any further," she says as she smiles behind her mask. "Because of COVID-19 restrictions, we can only allow a certain number of people into the park."

I looked at her angrily and say, "So I can't go in?!"

Calmly, she replies, "No, we're already at capacity." I can hear music coming from inside the park and people are standing all around.

Disappointed and confused, I decide not to argue with the woman and find a spot outside the park to listen to the speech. The area is shaded by a tree leaning from inside the park. So, I still have shade, but I'm not happy I have to stay out here. I want to be in the thick of things, even if this isn't what I expected. Even though I'm disappointed about where I have to stand, it's not like I'm standing out here alone. Looking to my left and then my right, I realize the sidewalk is full of people who can't go in, just like me. Thinking about the situation for a while, I realize it doesn't really matter if I'm inside or outside, as long as I'm here for the march and inevitable riot.

I station myself on the sidewalk with other protesters watching from afar. The speaker sounds like a Sunday morning preacher. He talks about a unity of the races and praying for our nation. With a look of disbelief, I turn to my neighbor and say, "What is all this? I thought there was going to be a protest today. Am I in the wrong place?"

The woman looked at me and smiled, saying, "No honey, you're in the right place. This is a demonstration organized by the Christian community leaders in Atlanta."

"Oh, I didn't know that," I reply.

The man on stage begins to shout at the crowd. "We can beat this! We can overcome hatred, because God is our strength!" As I look around at the people standing around me and in the park, everyone is smiling and saying, "Amen." I can tell they're smiling because I can see curves on their faces through the masks and their eyes lighting up. Do these people realize how serious this situation is? They're laid-back, drinking water, singing and dancing. Is this the way we need to deal with violence we didn't instigate? This isn't our fault! I know what God teaches… to turn the other cheek and forgive our transgressors, but how can we do that when the police won't let us? They keep us down and harass black people wherever we go. We can't ever feel safe as long as they're left unchecked!

The preacher goes on with his sermon talking about unity and community involvement and everyone is very responsive to what he has to say, but I'm growing impatient. He finally leaves the stage, then music starts playing again. I look at the stage and see a band playing church hymns. Everyone joins in and begins to sing, myself included. Growing up in the church, when you hear that music playing, you can't help joining in.

"I know this song. It's *How Great Thou Art*," I say before I sing along.

> *"Then sings my soul, my Savior God to Thee*
> *How great Thou art, how great though art*
> *Then sings my soul, my Savior God to Thee*
> *How great Thou art, how great Thou art…"*

After that song, a different speaker comes up on stage and starts his speech. He says much of the same things as the other preacher.

This is nice, but how much longer are the speeches going to last? I think to myself. I have been standing here listening to him and others for what seems like hours. Sure enough, I look at my phone and two hours have passed. This has turned out to be a pretty uneventful protest. These are good people, but I don't think I belong here. I don't want to belong here. When I left home, I had a specific goal in mind and this isn't it. I don't want to stand around with people hoping for peace on earth, but don't want to get their hands dirty! I want to take action and play a significant role in bringing justice to the black people who have died. This is a mess. What do I do now?

As I'm about to leave, I hear faint chanting from down the street. I turn around and see a group of people marching down the road chanting, "No justice, no peace! No justice, no peace!" Excitement washes over my whole body. Finally, someone is taking action and doing something! Oh, that's right, today is Juneteenth. There are a bunch of protests happening today. I know I'll be able to find protesters who want to take action. These people can pray—we need that too—but I want to be more involved than that.

The protesters are getting closer and I can see their masked faces. Most of them are black and they look so determined and focused. I think I like these people. As the group goes by, I jump into the line and start chanting with them. I've never felt so alive. I knew it would be this way. I'm standing side by side with people who look like me and feel the same way I do. Now the future is looking just a little bit brighter.

CHAPTER SIX

Marching down the street chanting, "Black lives matter!" I finally feel like I'm participating in something bigger than me. It's hot marching on the street, but there is a cool breeze blowing as I step farther away from the park. The street is full of protesters, and after a block or two, the police usher us to the left sidewalk. I pass by the National Center for Civil and Human Rights building and I feel a sense of irony that a Black Lives Matter march is happening right in front of it. History is repeating itself, and once again, it takes people dying for the nation to start paying attention. If national leaders really cared about human rights, this march wouldn't be necessary.

Controlling my emotions, I continue walking past the center. *Will this really work? The voice of the people isn't loud enough. Even this march is moving too quietly. I wonder if the protest will get louder once we reach City Hall. I'll hold on to hope until we get there.*

After walking for about thirty minutes, I find myself next to an older black man who looks like he might be having a hard time. I wave to get his attention and he kindly looks up. "Hello, are you doing okay?"

"Oh yeah, I'm just fine," he says. At that moment, I notice how hot I am. I feel the hot sun beaming on the back of my neck. Sweat is running down my back and it hits me; I forgot my umbrella in my car. I noticed the beads of sweat on the man's forehead. He has to be as hot as I am, maybe more, since he's been marching longer than me.

"It's pretty hot today," I say, breathing heavier as we make our way up a steep incline in the road. The man looks at me with a face that, despite his mask, makes me feel so welcome. Being around him reminds me of just how long it's been since I've seen my own family. I missed the last family reunion, and this man reminds me so much of my family. I can't help but feel a small connection to him. He begins to talk, and it snaps me out of my thoughts.

"You're right about that, young lady. We're definitely feelin' Atlanta heat today, but that's alright. Today is too important not to be out here."

I nod my head in agreement. "I completely agree with you on that. I hope everyone can see that for themselves."

"Well, I don't think they'd be out here if they didn't. This whole group here left work today to participate in this march," the man said.

Surprised, I ask, "You all work together?"

"We sure do, but don't worry. Our boss knows we're out here. In fact, they let us go with their blessin'." The man looks at me again and says, "My name is Simon. What's yours?"

"My name is Kiara. Nice to meet you!" It's nice to talk to someone who seems so kind. I don't know where we're going, so I decide to ask Simon. "Simon, is this march going to City Hall?"

Simon looks at me with a puzzled expression. Finally, he starts talking, but they are words I don't want to hear. "Oh no, Kiara. We've already been to City Hall, and now we're on our way back."

"Really! I missed the riot?"

"Riot!" Simon says sharply. "There was no riot. This is a peaceful protest. We don't need all that violence here in our city! Not again. We're still tryin' to repair the city from the riot from two days ago. No, we don't need that again," he says with a frown. I can see his eyes start to droop down and look tired. So, that must be why the stores still have their windows boarded up and the streets are so empty.

I look at Simon and ask, "Why do you look so sad, Simon? I know a lot of property damage can happen with a riot, but people are hurting, and extreme violence begets extreme violence."

Simon gives me a puzzled look again. I want him to say something. I want him to tell me

I'm right and to encourage me to go and fight, but by the look he's giving me, I don't believe that will happen. Simon finally looks at me with disappointment in his eyes and says, "So, you think the only way to win is with violence, do you? That tells me you've never been in a riot before, have you?"

"No," I say in a low voice.

"It's like nothin' you've ever seen before."

"I've seen it on the news."

"No," he says, shaking his head. "Watching it on TV is nothin' like actually bein' there. People runnin' and screamin'. The air was so thick with tear gas, you couldn't breathe. There were fires and explosions happenin' right in front of you. The police grabbin' whoever they could and throwin' 'em in a van to be taken off to jail. People who were perfectly sane a minute ago, actin' like they lost their minds, and no one could tell you why the madness wouldn't stop. I don't know if change can come after a night like that, but I do know that goin' through a night of chaos will change a person… and not for the better."

I can't believe what I'm hearing. His story is frightening and captivating at the same time. "Simon, how do you know all that?" I ask with dismay.

"Because I lived through the Rodney King riots in Los Angeles. I never wanted to go through that again, so I moved here to Atlanta," he says sadly. "But them riots seem to have followed me, and you wanna be a part of *that*?"

Simon's words cut right through me and I look at him, not knowing what to say. I can't believe that after all the death, this is what I'm hearing. "Simon!" I say sharply. "I can't believe you don't get what's happening here. A message needs to be sent. Police have to know that we are tired of being victimized. How can you say a riot doesn't bring change? It was on all the news stations and in all the papers. The government can't ignore the masses crying out in one voice, 'Mess with us and we'll mess with you.'" *Simon, please hear me*, I think to myself, but he doesn't.

Simon looks at me and shakes his head. Then with a sigh, he says, "And after the riot is over, do you think when you look around, you will find healing? No, there is cryin', sadness and destruction. You really need to stop and think if that path is truly the one you wanna be on, Kiara."

After that, Simon moves on, while I linger at the back of the march. What did he mean by that? Am I on the right path? Of course I am! The police are the enemy! They need a wake-up call… don't they? I can't believe I've come all this way to be let down like this. What am I supposed to do now? As I preoccupy my mind with these thoughts, I overhear two women talking about another protest.

"They're meeting on a street corner in Cabbagetown," a woman says.

"Yeah, I hear those people are pretty lively," the other woman says.

That's it! Finally, some people who understand how I feel. I flag down the two women and ask if they know the exact address of the protest.

"Oh yeah, it's on the corner of Baker Dr and Sunset N.W., but it doesn't start for a few hours," the woman says with bright eyes.

"Great!" I say with the most enthusiasm I've felt all day.

I leave the march and turn to go back the way I came, when I hear the women say, "You have yourself a good time!" *A good time?* Why would she say that? According to Simon, I won't have a good time; I could potentially be running from officers and fires. Well, maybe those women just don't see a riot as a bad thing. I know I don't. Sometimes you have to shake things up to get the wheels of change moving. Besides, I want to get right in those cops' faces and say, 'See me, hear me! I am a human being and I deserve to live just as much as you do!' It's nice to know there are others who feel the same as I do. For a minute there, I thought I was all alone. I'll go to this other protest and finally feel justified in coming here.

CHAPTER SEVEN

My legs are tired, but I walk as quickly as possible to my car. Wow, the heat combined with this long distance is starting to get to me. I pass by Olympic Park, expecting to see it full of protesters listening to another speech, but the park is empty. *Where did everyone go?* I guess they did eventually start marching. It's okay that I missed it. They're not interested in protesting how I want to protest anyway. Yeah, this is fine. They can do it their way and I can do it my way.

I finally make it to my car and start the AC as soon I get in. I grab my water bottle and start drinking, letting the water run down the sides of my mouth. I have no idea how hot it is, but the AC hitting me in the face right now is helping. I hope Simon is okay. He was sweating just as bad as I was. According to him, they were all heading back, so I'm sure their march is over by now. So he should be resting, and in some place cool.

"Okay, now what?" I have a few hours to kill and not a clue how. Just then, I hear a growl from my stomach. That's right, I haven't had anything to eat. Great, I'll go grab me something to eat! This is Atlanta, so there has to be plenty of places to eat. I'm in the mood for Asian food, and I know exactly where to go. A place where the food is so good, even if you're full, you never want to stop eating. The restaurant is in Asian Square in Doraville. I've been to Asian Square before, and that mall has some really good places to eat. It takes me a while to get there. I guess it would help if I stopped getting turned around.

After entering the square, I drive to the back and see the restaurant I went to the last time I was here. They serve Korean and Vietnamese food there, and the atmosphere is always nice. Before I walk into the restaurant, I can smell the yummy flavors of the food. Mmm… I smell ginger and spices; it's making my mouth water with anticipation. I can't wait to taste their yummy food. When I step inside, I see there aren't many people here. I'm glad, now I don't have to wait for a table.

A man with a charming smile walks up to me and says, "Hello, how many people are with you today?"

"Hello, it's just me. Do you have a small table by a window?" I ask, smiling back.

"Because of COVID, that's all we have right now."

"Oh, that's right, I forgot my mask in my car!"

The man laughs. "It's okay, I sometimes forget mine too. Come with me and I'll show you to your table."

When I sit down, the man gives me a menu and walks away. Looking around the room, I see how everyone is spread apart and I start to feel a little better about not having my mask on. It isn't long before the waitress arrives.

"Hello, can I get you a drink?"

"Hello, I'll just have a glass of water, no lemon," I say.

"Okay, I'll be right back with that," she says with a smile. I look over the menu for something quick to order. I don't need to spend too much time here. I'll need plenty of time to get to the protest on that street corner. The food here looks really good. I think I'm in the mood for pork. They have a delicious roast pork with rice and greens. I'm so hungry, just thinking about it is making my stomach growl. I hope the waitress comes back soon; I'm ready to order.

Not long after that thought, I see the waitress coming my way. She sits my water on the table and asks, "Are you ready to order, or do you need some more time?"

Excited, I reply, "Oh, I don't need more time. I'd like the pork lunch with greens."

The waitress smiles and says, "Okay, I'll get that out to you right away."

I can hear a couple talking at the table to the right of me. They are a black couple talking about the killing of a black man two days ago. The woman sounds scared, and the man is trying to act like it's just how things are.

"This keeps happening around here. Maybe we should move to another state," the woman says.

"I don't think that will make a difference. Racism is everywhere, so we might as well stay where we are," the man replied. I guess this topic is unavoidable. It is Juneteenth, and protests are happening all over the country. I want to say something to them, but the woman doesn't look like she will respond well to, 'Why don't you join a protest?' I feel like I should say *something* though. Maybe I can tell them what I'm doing and that might encourage them to do it too. I'll try to sound really sincere. I lean over as far as I can and try to get their attention.

"Um, excuse me? I know you're having a private conversation, but I want you to know that I was feeling helpless myself. So, I decided to join a protest. That's why I'm in Georgia today.

You don't have to go that route, but it helps me cope with what's going on to participate in the marches."

The two stop and look at me for a few seconds, but honestly, the silence is choking me. Finally, the man says, "I'm glad you have an outlet for your frustration, but I'm not interested in protesting. Life has been this way for years. You should know nothing ever changes. It doesn't matter who is in office or which political party is in the house, this is the reality of our lives."

"Maybe now, but it doesn't have to stay this way. You may not live to see it, and I may not live to see it, but change will happen as long as we never stop fighting for it," I say.

"So, you're fighting for your children, or your children's children? That's great, but that doesn't help us at all."

"Being a part of that change is what helps us," I say, trying to hold back my anger. What is with this guy? He can't see the big picture. I know everyone isn't going to think the same way I do, but I can't believe other black people would not want to get involved in their own movement. This is our problem. Why is he against protesting? I want to ask him, but I can tell he no longer wants to talk.

At that moment, the waitress appears with my order, and I turn around to see the food set in front of me. It looks and smells heavenly, but as hungry as I am, I can't bring myself to eat it. Suddenly, I feel a soft touch on my shoulder. When I look up, I see the woman from before. She looks at me and says softly, "Thank you." Then I watch her and the man walk out the door. I guess one of them listened to what I had to say. I wasn't trying to give a speech, but that guy just wasn't hearing me. I'm glad the woman found some comfort in my words, though. Maybe she'll get involved, despite that guy's opinion.

I can't help but smile and hope they're alright. I lower my head and say a little prayer for them and the meal before me. With an *amen*, I dive into my lunch. With the first bite, I go to a place of bliss. The pork is so tender and juicy it melts in my mouth. The spices are so rich, I can taste them with every bite. I'm so glad I came here to eat!

While I'm eating, I think about the upcoming protest and how I can make the most of the experience. First, I will try and find a group who is really into it and join in with them. Since this is my first riot, I don't want to suddenly find myself alone. Then, I'll get as close as I can to the officers so they can see the look on my face when I shout, 'You'll listen to me now!' I don't like to use profanity, so I'll keep it clean.

Even though I know this is serious, I can't help giggling to myself. This is the most exciting thing I've ever done in my life. I hope everything goes well and people stay safe, because that's important too. Simon said it was chaos and people were everywhere screaming. The thought runs a chill down my back and makes me pause from enjoying my food. I know that was his experience, but that doesn't always happen. Hopefully this time, there'll be yelling and maybe some minor damage, but the people will disperse after the officers get serious. I don't want anyone to get hurt. The point is to be heard and seen as people with a cause. That's what really matters.

I finish my meal and check the clock on my phone. Wow, it's two o'clock! I guess it took me longer to get here than I thought. It's okay, the protest starts at five, so I'm still fine. The waitress appears at my table to gather my dishes and asks, "Would you care for dessert?"

"Sure," I say. "I think I have time for that." The waitress smiles and hands me the dessert menu. "Wow, everything looks good," I say, possibly a little too loud. The menu is full of Asian pastries that look like something out of an anime. There are strawberry tarts and crème brûlée that look so tasty it's hard to hold in my enthusiasm. I look up at the waitress and exclaim, "I'll have the crème brûlée, please."

"Okay, I'll get that right out to you," she says with a smile.

While I'm waiting for my dessert, I think of where I can go to kill two hours. While I'm thinking, the waitress returns with my crème brûlée. "This looks great," I say as the waitress puts the dessert on the table in front of me. The waitress smiles and returns to the back of the restaurant. I pull out my phone and search for nearby attractions. Hmm, it looks like there's a farmers' market in Johns Creek. It might be fun to look around there for a while, since there's some time before the protest starts. Who knows, maybe there'll be some like-minded people there I can talk to.

CHAPTER EIGHT

I finish my dessert and pay the waitress for my meal. Before she walks away, I ask her about the area the market is in. "Excuse me, do you know the town of Johns Creek?"

"Yes, it's a really nice area."

"Oh good, I was thinking about going there for a little while. I'm attending a protest in a couple of hours and need to kill time somewhere."

"Oh, you're one of the protesters from another state, aren't you?"

"Yes." I don't know why, but the look she's giving me makes me feel uncomfortable. "Do you not like people from other states protesting in Georgia?"

"As long as they behave themselves, I don't mind at all." And with that, she walks away and returns to the back of the restaurant. I wonder what that was all about. Oh well, I'm not here to cause trouble, at least not any trouble that will hurt anyone.

I left the restaurant with the waitress' words on my mind. These protests have a purpose and a goal. I hope people can understand that. While driving to Johns Creek, I try to put the waitress' words into perspective. I forgot a riot had just broken out downtown only two days ago. Maybe she believes people from out of town started the violence or were with the ones who did. I should've asked more questions, but she seemed so judgmental. I was intimidated by the looks she was giving me. I want to be mad and insulted, but perhaps the wounds of that night are still fresh and slow to heal for her. I don't want to insult her by telling her not all protesters want to cause trouble. I'll just have to show her, and anyone else who expects the worst, that I'm not here to cause trouble.

I make it to Johns Creek and head for the market. I think this market is supposed to be pretty big. It should have a large variety of teas there. Maybe I can find some to take back home with me. I do enjoy my tea, and herbal teas are my favorite. I can't wait to get there. With the help of the GPS, I find the market. Looking at it from the parking lot, I see the market isn't big, it's huge! I've never seen a farmer's market this big, not even in downtown Nashville. I quickly find a parking spot, put on my mask, and go inside.

Wow, I thought this place was huge from the outside, but it looks even bigger from the inside. Stepping through the front door, there is a sea of fruit right in front of me. First, there are mangos and papaya, and right beside them are lemons, limes and star fruit. Behind them are some fruits I've never seen before. I move to the back of the market, and I find rows of vegetables and nuts. I love pecans; I think I'm going to get some. I make a beeline for the nuts behind the vegetables on the right and find them almost immediately. *These look really good, and the price is good too*. This same amount of pecans would be double the price back home.

I look around, going from aisle to aisle, and I finally find the row of tea and coffee I was hoping to find. There are so many, I can't believe the variety. I see some herbal teas and look for my favorite; liver-mind herbal tea. This tea is good for you, and it tastes great too. Most herbal teas I've tried taste like dirt in hot water, but this tea tastes really good. This stuff makes me feel good too. I think I'll get two boxes.

Walking to the next aisle, I see two Caucasian men talking and laughing among themselves. I approach where they're standing slowly, making sure I don't look directly at them. It's strange, but I feel really uncomfortable right now. When I pass them by, I see what they're laughing at and my heart sinks. The two men are looking at a label on a bag of chocolates. The label has a black girl on it eating some of the chocolate. She is dark-skinned, and one of the men says, "doodoo brown," and laughs even louder.

I stop and look at the men with a cutthroat look in my eyes. When they notice me, they immediately stop laughing, which means nothing. What are they thinking, making comments like that? Did they really think no one would hear them? They are surrounded by people of color, and they're still comfortable making racist remarks like that. I didn't want to, but all the racist comments that have ever been addressed at me come flooding back to me. Random people I didn't know would ask me if I wanted some watermelon or fried chicken for lunch. These two have done nothing but fuel my determination to wake people up and show them the result of their stupid comments. That is the reason protesting is needed. People like them have no idea how their stupid comments affect other people. They need to be shown they are wrong.

I continue walking down the aisle and around the corner until I can no longer hear their voices. I look at the clock on my phone. It's almost time to go, so I think I'll go ahead and check out. I don't want to stay in the store anymore anyway. After what just happened, I'm ready to go. It's a shame, there is so much more to see. Walking toward the checkout line, I see an aisle full of drinks and another with noodles and ramen bowls. I want to see more, but I guess I shouldn't waste any more time here. I'll remember this place and come back another time. Maybe then the visit will be more pleasant.

After checking out, I leave the market with my tea and head for my car. Holding back my tears of frustration, I try to make it to my car without screaming. I won't stop until people like them see themselves for the narrow-minded people they are. What gives them the right to say something like that and just expect me to accept it? So why didn't I say something? I didn't want to make a scene. Crap, all that means is that I was afraid of them. I don't want to be afraid; I want to teach them I don't have to be afraid. That's what the protests are going to do. Speaking of the protests, I need to get going. My feet were heavy when I began the walk to my car, but they are light as a feather now. I get to my car, hop inside, and head out for Cabbagetown. This is going to be an epic experience.

CHAPTER NINE

The drive to the street corner is short, only about thirty minutes. I guess I'm still upset over what happened at the store; my foot was a little heavy on the gas pedal. I'm at the protest a little early, so I linger in my car for a while. I see there are only a few people here, and again there are too many white people. I don't have anything against white people; I just don't know why they're out here protesting. Maybe they have black friends they're supporting. I can understand that, but I don't want them trying to take over. This is a black problem, so black people should be the ones to solve it. Still, where are the black people? There were a lot of them at the protest at Olympic

Park. It could be they only wanted to go to one protest today, and that was the one they chose. Yeah, that makes sense. Still, I hope I won't be the only one out here. I'm new at this, and I don't want to be the only black person here.

I gather my courage, put on my mask, and slowly step out of my car. I'm bursting with excitement and my stomach is full of butterflies as I approach one of the protesters and say, "Hello."

The woman turns to me and gives me a big smile. "Hi, welcome," she says, eyes beaming. She, and everyone else on the corner, is also wearing a mask. These people are really nice. I guess it doesn't matter that they're white; we're all working toward the same goal after all. I just wish more black people were here. Just then, I notice a black woman with an African T-shirt step out of her car. Yes! I'm so happy to see her! Okay, I won't be alone here, thank goodness!

The black woman walks right up to me and says, "Hello, do you have a sign?"

Oh my goodness! I forgot to make a sign! "Oh no, I don't have one," I say nervously.

The woman doesn't hesitate. She hands me her sign and says, "You can hold this one."

"Thank you," I say. "So, when is the protest going to start?"

"Right now," she says with an obvious smile under her black mask. Right then, she picks up a boom box and sits it on top of a large metal garbage can. The music she plays is uplifting and promotes unity among people. I look around and all the people, who have surprisingly grown in number, are dancing and holding their signs up to all the cars driving by. The corner has a traffic light in front of it. Across the street, I can see people holding signs and dancing to the music. This protest is not on one street corner, it's on all four of the street corners.

Most of the protesters are white, but there are black people mixed in. Cars are driving by and honking their horns in support, and that is where I see a lot of black people. Why don't they get out and join us? It's then I remember what that man said in the restaurant.

'I'm glad you have an outlet for your frustration, but I'm not interested in protesting. Life has been this way for years. You should know nothing ever changes. It doesn't matter who is in office or which political party is in the house, this is the reality of our lives.'

How many black people feel that way? There must be a way to bring them into the fold. Maybe this is the way. The more of us they see participating, the more they'll want to join us… I hope. Yeah, lead by example.

I look around at all the protesters and start realizing something. Wait, what is going on? They're not marching. They're not even shouting anything. They're dancing with their signs in the air. Right then it dawns on me, once again. I AM AT THE WRONG DEMONSTRATION!

Oh no, how did this happen again? I misunderstood what those women were saying. They didn't mean have fun yelling at cops, they meant, have fun dancing with a sign in your hands. How is this protesting, anyway? Where is the aggression? Where is the opposition? I know there is peaceful protesting, but this is so peaceful it's more like a dance party. What message are they trying to send? Do they really think they can beat racism with music and dancing? I never realized there are so many different ways to protest, and I think I'm seeing them all today. But that also means the protest I'm looking for must be going on somewhere too. I just have to find it.

CHAPTER TEN

I can't believe this. What am I going to do now? With the music blaring in my ear, I look up to see white people and black people dancing and laughing together. They look so happy; I can't help but smile. They are older people, around late 40s and older. Look at them having no trouble at all getting along with each other. Has my scope been too narrow?

Right at that moment, I hear a familiar song. Is that…? It is. I remember this song from my childhood. My mom and dad listened to this song. It was part of car sing-a-longs when we took road trips. This song used to make me and my sisters laugh and feel lighthearted. I can't believe I'm standing here on a street corner with total strangers listening to *Ebony and Ivory*. I look up at the black lady who shared her sign with me. She's looking at me while I'm looking at her. I can't hold it in anymore. Looking at the woman, I begin to laugh. I laugh with delight and irony. I laugh until tears form in the corner of my eyes. And like a virus, the laughter spreads to everyone at the protest. I even see people in their cars stopping at the traffic light laughing as well. This is crazy, but I can't help myself. The environment of this protest is so lighthearted. I feel really comfortable with these people.

After the laugh fest ends, I shout, "Black lives matter!" and dance while shaking my sign. This is okay for now, and I can ask them if they know of another protest happening tonight. I don't know why, but I feel so happy and welcomed by these people. We're all out here sharing our pain and joy; it feels like a community. A community with moves! I look to my left and then my right. People are dancing together and by themselves, all the while holding their signs to everyone passing by.

The signs to my left say *Black Lives Matter* and *Vote Like Your Life Depends on It!* And the signs to my right say *We Stand With You*, and another one has four different color hands joining together. Is that what the white people are saying? If we stand united, we can bring social change, or that this is what social unity is supposed to look like? Either way is better than what *I've* seen in society. The people in this community really have the right attitude about social equality.

Looking around at the diverse crowd, my curiosity gets the better of me. I turn to one of the white women standing next to me. "Hi," I say with a smile. "Why are you supporting the Black Lives Matter movement?"

The woman looks at me with pain in her eyes and says, "Because I want to do more than complain about what is happening in our community. My name is Anita, by the way. What's yours?"

"Oh sorry, my name is Kiara. I'm from Tennessee. So, everyone here is from this community?"

"Yes," she says, beaming, "and the turnout today is more than I expected."

Feeling courageous, I confess, "I'm surprised to see so many, um…"

"White people?" Anita says with a wry smile under her mask.

"Well, yes," I say sheepishly. "I'm not opposed to it, I just didn't expect it."

"That's okay," Anita says, gently squeezing my arm. "All of us here have our own reasons, but we know that if we want the world to change for the better, we all must join together and say, 'Enough.'" Wow, I never thought I'd see a white person of Anita's age say something like that. It's been my experience that people of the younger generation are more supportive of equality for all, but not the Baby Boomers. "We meet out here every weekday for one hour to protest and raise awareness in the community. Most people support us and honk as they go by. Some people don't, but we'll keep coming out here either way."

Anita is pretty amazing. Not wanting her to stop talking, I decide to ask her a few more questions. "Anita, what do you want to come from all this? I mean, you must have a goal, right?" As if my question lit a fire in Anita, she turns to me and begins to speak with enthusiasm that is a little scary.

"Oh, I want new laws against racism, accountability for police who commit racist crimes, and I want awareness brought to the issue so people can no longer say racism doesn't exist!" I can't believe what I'm hearing. I stand in shock at what Anita is saying. Who *is* this woman? She wants the exact same things I do! I feel my eyes well up with tears, but I fight to keep it together. She's only one of many, and those odds are not too promising.

Right then, another woman sidesteps her way over to me and Anita. "Hi, my name is Katherine, but you can call me Kat. I heard what you two were talking about, and I couldn't help coming over to hear more." Kat is an older woman around the age of 65, but she really has a lot of energy. She's been dancing the whole time without a sign of tiring. With a smile behind her mask, she chimes in on our conversation. "I'm sorry to just barge in, but I was drawn in by your topic. I think we need more conversations like this if we're going to move forward as a community."

"No, it's alright," I say with a smile. "I would love to hear what you have to say." I'm nervous that I'm drawing so much attention, but I can't help being excited too. I look at Kat to ask her a question, but she starts talking before I can speak.

"I want these protests to unite the people, not divide them," she says with tears in her eyes.

With my own tears welling up, I say, "That's an admirable goal, but from what I've seen, the police are the problem. The police, and the ones who look the other way when they commit murder."

Kat looks at me with soft eyes and says, "Education is what's needed for police, so they can better understand the black community and how they feel about them."

Education? "What could they possibly learn that will replace their instincts to shoot first and ask questions later?" Kat is too idealistic. Does she actually believe officers will care enough to put what they are taught to use?

"Getting to know the community you serve is a way to educate them," Kat says softly. I know she's trying to be helpful, but I just can't believe any officer, unless they come from there, would bother getting to know a black community! Kat, reading the expression on my face, looks at me like she has something to say. "Kiara, why don't you join us for our community meeting? The demonstration is going to end soon, so why don't you join us?"

"Kat, I appreciate your invite, but I don't know if that's a good idea."

Kat, with determination in her voice, says, "You look like the type who wants to see the whole picture before you make up your mind. I would love for you to join us, and then we can finish our talk with the whole group present."

Wow, this woman doesn't know me at all. My mind is already made up. I don't need her to convince me of anything. In the end, it's just a white person's opinion about a black person's problem. But she is being really nice to me; I don't know if she'll be as open to what I have to say as she is to what she has to say. I guess I can go if she'll let me speak too, if only to show her that black people can be open-minded. I may not agree with everything she's saying, but that doesn't mean what she's saying isn't worth listening to. Ugh, do I really want to go to a meeting surrounded by a bunch of people I don't know?

Over the next few minutes, I take in the surrounding backdrop of what's going on around me. The street corner is full of graffiti and people are standing with a gravel parking lot behind them, with an old street in need of repair in front of them. People are selling Black Lives Matter T-shirts and caps in the gravel parking lot. I see African artwork leaning up against a single run-down building on the edge of the lot. The artwork is very colorful; I like it. It's all ethnic pieces with a 60s vibe to it. It doesn't look like anyone is watching them. Maybe they are participating in the demonstration? Oh well, I didn't come here to buy artwork.

I look at the people and how happy and determined they are. You can see the hope on their faces; the hope for change. These people brought their children to the protest too. I hope they're teaching them how important this moment truly is.

I turn to Kat and Anita. "Okay, I'll go to your community meeting, but I might have to leave early." I still haven't found the right protest yet, and my time is running out; the sun will start setting soon. With excitement, Kat and Anita give me the address of the meeting. It will be at Kat's house, not too far from the street corner where we're at now. I'll stay long enough to finish our debate, and then I'll leave. I hope I can get Kat to see the police need to be reassessed, and the ones who have a history of excessive force need to be fired. That is the only way to make a real difference in the safety of everyone, not just black people.

The protest ends at the corner, and I look for the nice black lady who gave me her sign to use. I find her by the boombox, packing her things up. "Hello, thank you for letting me use your sign. I appreciate it. I guess I was a little unprepared."

"Oh, that's okay. I'm glad you joined us tonight."

"Well, I guess I'll see you at the community meeting tonight. My name is Kiara, by the way."

"Oh, my name is Roberta. So, you're going to the meeting? That's great. It will be nice to have someone there with a different take on social equality." Roberta has a confident look in her eyes. She is nice and likes to help people, whether she knows them or not. She reminds me a lot of my mom.

"Yeah, Kat and I are in the middle of a debate on what would work best for police reform."

Roberta raises an eyebrow before she speaks. "Kat is very outspoken, and she has some good ideas, but I don't think she's truly capable of putting herself in the shoes of the black community."

"I was thinking that myself, but I didn't want to dismiss what she has to say." Roberta is a breath of fresh air. She's so calm when she speaks, but I can feel her intensity. "Will you be at the meeting, Roberta?"

"Oh yes, I'll be there," she says with a smile.

"Okay, I'll see you there. Save me a seat."

"You got it, Kiara. It's nice to meet you. And don't get discouraged. We're out here because we still have hope change is coming."

With that, I wave goodbye to Roberta and head for my car. It's not far from where I'm standing, so I get there quickly. Pulling out the address to Kat's house, I exhale heavily. I had my reservations about going to this meeting, but after talking to Roberta, I'm feeling a little better. I hope they get right to the discussion, because I need to begin my search again. There must be a more involved protest out here today. Maybe they're waiting for nightfall before they begin. I won't stop looking until the day is completely over. I have to have hope that I'll find one.

CHAPTER ELEVEN

I arrive at Kat's house and notice the sun starting to set. I quickly knock on the door and Kat answers it.

"Welcome, Kiara. Come right in. We'll be starting the meeting soon." Kat's mask is off, so I can see her whole face now. Her face is bright-looking with the wrinkles someone would get if they smiled all the time. When she smiles at me, I can't help but smile back. Kat is a little overbearing, but I *do* like her.

I look around the room. Some people are wearing masks, and some are not. All the people from the protest, excluding Roberta, are here, along with two police officers. Where is

Roberta? She said she would be here. What are officers doing here? I didn't expect it, but I'm not comfortable around these officers. What do they hope to accomplish by being around people who are blaming them for the death of someone? I'm sorry, but this seems pointless to me. What if I'm missing out on a real demonstration while I'm wasting my time here? A demonstration with people who want to speak out with action, not just words! Crap, I don't want to be here!

I start to head for the door when, as if she can read my mind, Kat grabs my arm and says, "Oh look everyone, we have a new visitor to our meeting tonight!" Oh my goodness, how does she keep doing that? A nervous smile grows across my face, and I slowly follow Kat through the living room. Really, does she have to parade me in front of everyone? Kat clears her throat and says, "Good evening, everyone. This is Kiara, from Tennessee, and she'll be joining us for our meeting tonight."

I let out a sigh. "Hello. I'm not from your community. I heard about your demonstration and decided to join you. I hope that's okay with everyone." I glance over at the officers standing by the door. I look for some kind of expression on their faces, but all I see is indifferent smiles. I wonder if these officers are friends of these people. Kat introduces me to the people in the room.

"Kiara, you already know Anita, and this is Adel and Clare. They are regulars at the protests on the corner. These two are Stephanie and Rachel; they just started attending the protests last week." Their smiles are pleasant, and I do feel more comfortable here after meeting everyone.

"Kat, where is Roberta? I thought she was going to be here."

"Oh, Roberta is going to be late. She has to make sure her family eats dinner." Oh no, I wish she would have said that back at the corner. Of course, if she had, I probably would have skipped coming here.

After her explanation, Kat moves on to the officers. A woman and a man with slim builds and a calm demeanor stand statuesque at the door. Both are Caucasian and seem to be happy to be here. I know I'm being closed minded, but I can't bring myself to smile back. Why are they here anyway? Do they want to explain what happened from an officer's point of view? This whole meeting is confusing and weird.

It's then that Kat walks me over to the officers standing by the door. With a smile on her face, she says, "Hello Officer Patterson, Officer Reeves. This is Kiara."

"Hello. It's nice to meet you, Kiara," Patterson says with a grin.

"Yes, it's good to see you here," Reeves adds. To me, Reeves looks more into this than Patterson, because she turned to me and dove a little deeper. "Kiara, how did you end up at a protest in Georgia?" This is way too convenient; they must be hiding something from these people. I'm going to test them and see what happens.

"Actually," I say to Reeves, "to take your job away." Reeves looks at me in complete shock.

Patterson looks at me with absolute disdain. "I knew it," I say faintly under my breath. I knew they were only here for show.

I hear Kat behind me, but I don't look at her till she moves to stand in front of me. With an intense look in her eyes, she says, "Kiara, listen, that's not why we're here tonight. We gather after the demonstration to talk about what is needed to invoke real change in our community. I want our community to unite and work with police officers. I'm determined to do my part to stop the killing of black people." Out of nowhere, Kat begins to cry. Anita and several others come and surround Kat and hug her. I'm completely confused right now. What is she doing? Why is she crying? Look at all these people coming to console her. What has she gone through that would justify these tears? I wonder if the same thing would happen if I started crying. Are the tears of a black woman any less moving than the tears of a white woman? No one is even asking me why I said what I said. Is this really what the struggle for our social equality is supposed to look like?

Officer Reeves steps forward. "Kat's right, and as police officers, we need to get to know the communities we serve. That's why Officer Patterson and I are here tonight." I look at Officer Reeves and I can see the desperation on her face, and I kinda feel bad about what I said. Then, I look at Officer Patterson, his eyes full of suspicion and hate… and I don't feel bad anymore. I want to ask Officer Patterson why he came to the meeting. I want to know if my suspicions about him are true. Except if I start talking to him, I don't think I could hold my anger back. Officers like him are the reason meetings like this are happening. Officers like him are the reason the protests are needed. He's nothing but part of the problem.

Reeves looks like she truly wants to move in a positive direction in this community, but Patterson looks like someone forced him to be here. The question is, how many officers in this community think like Reeves and how many think like Patterson? That will determine how much change, if any, happens in Cabbagetown. These meetings are good to clear the air and discuss what the people want, but real change rarely happens from people talking.

To lift the heaviness in the air, Anita speaks up. "Okay everyone, we're going to get started. Our first topic tonight is, should we organize a community over-watch committee?"

Before Anita can continue, Kat moves to the front of the room and says, "Before that, Anita, let's all gather around and pray." Anita smiles and starts moving in to hold hands with her. It isn't long before the entire group has moved in close to hold hands. Not in a circle—there isn't enough room for that—it's more like a jagged row of lines. I'm stunned at how everyone is so open about praying together. I grew up in a Christian home, but I must admit, I haven't really prayed about this at all. I look at Officer Reeves and she's smiling at me, holding out her hand for me to take. I take it, but I'm not all that comfortable touching her. She's the nice one though, so I don't want to seem like a jerk.

Officer Patterson isn't looking at me at all, but I can tell he looks just as uncomfortable as I am. He's standing so stiff; he looks like a cadaver on a slab. He holds hands with a group member on his right and Officer Reeves on his left. How did I end up so close to two people I would never be around under normal circumstances? I look at Officer Patterson one more time and I can't help but smile to myself. I think I can see a vein popping out on his forehead. He looks like he's truly hating this.

Great, our common ground is that we both need to pray more. That's weirdly simplistic. I guess if everyone prayed about social injustice, we wouldn't have such a huge mess on our hands. I can hear Anita and she has already started to pray. "Lord, come into this house tonight and guide our words. Let your will be done tonight. Let us find resolution and unity through your word. Thank you. In your glorious name, Jesus, we pray. Amen." The words rush over me like a wave, and I find myself wanting to find a way to make peace with Officer Patterson. I wish there was a way to resolve the conflict without violence.

My head rises, and I look at Officer Reeves, but then my phone goes off. When I look at it, I see an alert that reads, 'Protest gathering downtown. Police have put up barricades to keep protesters back. Everyone is encouraged to attend. Let's show the police we will not back down!' "This is it!" I say under my breath. This is what I have been waiting for. Finally, I found the right protest! I quickly let go of Reeves' hand and head for the door.

Reeves turns to me and whispers, "Do you really need to go?"

I look back at her with an unsure look on my face. "I… I do. I have to see this through to the end." And with that, I open the door and close it behind me.

CHAPTER TWELVE

After I close the door, I lean up against it and try to take some deep breaths. "Come on. In through the nose, out through the mouth." I don't want to abandon a peaceful solution, but I also need to face those cops who are not interested in peace. All they want is compliance, and that isn't good enough for the people. We want answers and justice for the families who have lost loved ones. What will happen to them if we talk and promises are made and nothing changes? We aren't politicians, we are the people of this country and we need to feel validated and heard. I don't need to talk myself into this; this is an easy decision for me to make. I know the people in this house feel as though they have the answer, but it's not as cut and dry for me and many others. I know this is something I want to be a part of.

Walking to my car, I look around and see the stars are out and the moon is high in the sky. I'm nervous and a little scared, but I'm also excited at the possibility of experiencing the high of telling a bunch of crooked cops off. I don't want to hurt them; I want to tell them how it feels to live with fear your whole life. How it feels to not know how someone will react when you approach them. Will they see you as a person, or will they rely on stereotypes and judge you before you say a word?

With a huge crowd of angry people coming at them, they'll be the ones afraid. I really don't want anyone to get hurt. I want them to open their eyes and see they can't get away with treating people like animals. The abuse of authority has to stop, and now they'll realize that someone is watching them. We are watching them. *I* am watching them. Now is the time to make our voices heard. This is going to be a life-changing moment for me. I know there'll be people there who'll probably want to start trouble, but I know how to take care of myself. I can avoid the ones who want to be violent.

My walk is slow, and my thoughts are on what this night means to me. I have a good life, and as far as I know, no one close to me has died due to an encounter with a police officer. But I still feel the pain of the ones who have. This issue has been debated in groups and with lawmakers in Washington. I don't want to sit this out and do nothing but talk about it. That's good for others, but not me! I'm angry and hurt by the way my people are treated. How we have been treated for generations. It has to change, and tonight is the beginning of my fight with the status quo of this nation!

It's a short walk to my car, but once I get there, a picture of the people at the community meeting pops into my head. Everyone is standing, holding hands, and praying together. It's such a serene picture, and with that on my mind, I feel my anger leaving me. I shake my head quickly as if to shake the picture until it falls out of my ears. I need to focus and get going. I don't want to miss this opportunity. So why am I thinking about that now? I don't even know these people and they don't know me either. I came to Georgia because I want to stand side by side with people who are as angry as I am. People who want to get up in the police's faces and make them see us. I finally found a protest that'll let me do that, so I'm not passing this up! God forgive me, I have to do this!

At that moment, my mind wanders to the moment I met Simon and what he said to me. *'Watching it on TV is nothin' like actually bein' there. People runnin' and screamin'. The air was so thick with tear gas, you couldn't breathe. There were fires and explosions happenin' right in front of you. The police grabbin' whoever they could and throwin' 'em in a van to be taken off to jail. People who were perfectly sane a minute ago, actin' like they lost their minds, and no one could tell you why the madness wouldn't stop.'* Those words begin to echo in my mind and I wonder if I really want to see that… NO! I can't run away now. That's why the black community is in so much trouble. We have to take a stand and make our voices known. It's been so many years since Bloody Sunday, so many years since the Freedom March, and nothing's changed. It's like we're on a hamster wheel that keeps spinning, but doesn't go anywhere. Prayer is good, talking is good, but right now, action is needed. Then why am I still standing at my car? With a sigh, I open my car door and get inside. I'll go to the protest, and if it is too dangerous, I'll leave. Yeah, that's what I'll do.

Safe in my resolution, I start my car and head to the address on the notification. It's actually not that far, only about ten minutes away. This address is closer to downtown Atlanta, so I'll be in a good spot to head back home when it's over. The events of the day weigh on my mind and my body. Looking at the road ahead of me makes my body feel heavy, and I feel as though I'm glued to my seat. The weight is heavy, but I'm also feeling really happy to be on this path. I have not accomplished much in my life and I need to be here. I want to make my life count for something. So, I will make my mark here, but this isn't the end. I will attend as many protests as I can. This is good. Everything will be okay and I will accomplish my goals. I'm traveling in the dark now, but I will be a beacon of light for the struggle of social injustice.

CHAPTER THIRTEEN

Driving down the highway, my stomach begins to fill with butterflies. But those butterflies turn to stones when I see the mass of people in the street ahead of me. Where do I park my car in this huge crowd? The people look so focused, and I think I see some photographers on a street corner. It's good to see the media here. That way, everything the cops do will be on camera. Maybe I can park in that direction. I move over to the street next to the media cameras and find a parking spot two blocks down. There are other cars parking here, so I believe I'm in the right spot.

I can't believe I finally made it! My head is light as I walk down the street to where the protesters are. *This is it!* I say to myself. As I reach my destination, the street is lit up by headlights in front of a line of about 20 police officers and bright flood lights from behind them. It's so loud, everyone is shouting at the same time. I can't hear myself think. I also notice some people are wearing masks and some are not. For safety, I think I'll put my mask on. I reach into my pocket and pull out my black mask. As I put it on, I'm really happy I decided to bring the black one. Everyone here wearing a mask has on a black one.

I look around to try and find a place in front of the officers, but there isn't one. Groups of protesters are lined up right in front of them. Every nook and cranny is full and there isn't anywhere for me to stand. I knew I was late, but I didn't think I was that late. There are people everywhere, and they're starting to get closer to the cops. This is so frustrating. I finally make my way to an 'in your face' protest, and all I'm doing is standing around. Maybe if I keep moving, I can find a spot to start participating.

I move to the middle of the street to try and get a better look at what's going on. I hear people around me shouting, "Black Lives Matter!" and "Stop killing us!" I look to my left and I see a man laughing. What is that? Oh no, I think he has a gun in his pants!

I turn to my right and a woman is crying uncontrollably, saying to herself, "It's not fair, we are people just like them." I feel so bad I almost forget about the guy with the gun. That is, until he fires it!

My head whips around so fast I thought I broke it. Then, without warning, three officers jump on the guy and wrestle him to the ground. Apparently, the man shot the gun in the air. I don't think he was going to hurt anyone, but that doesn't matter now. As I watch the man being taken away by the officers, all I can think about is, will he be treated well by the cops, or will he never be seen again? Okay, that is all the excitement I need tonight. But as I finish my thought, I hear people shouting from behind where I'm standing. As I turn around, I see protesters marching up the street toward me and the line of police officers.

A woman from the crowd yells at the police. "You killed my brother!"

People are standing right in front of the line of officers shouting, "No justice, no peace!" The police are just standing there doing nothing. Are they taking these people seriously or are they simply waiting for orders? I hear glass breaking next to me and I don't know how it started or who started it, but someone has set a car on fire! What was the point of that? Do they even know who that car belongs to? People are just standing around it, yelling profanities. The police issue a warning for everyone to disperse. I guess they've had enough. I can't believe this. I just got here and now I have to leave.

I move toward the street my car is parked on, when I realize something. No one is leaving. If anything, the police telling everyone to leave has fired the protesters up more. Is anyone going to listen to them? I don't think so. People in masks are breaking into a store down the street. Why are they doing that? That has nothing to do with protesting social injustice. Oh no, they've set it on fire! Will no one stop them? They're destroying someone else's dreams and hard work! Can't they see what they're doing is wrong? These people are clapping and whistling! Why are these people cheering at this destruction? I thought we were here to yell at police and make them see us!

There is smoke everywhere from the fires and it's getting hard to see what's going on. Simon was right, this is madness! I turn back around and see the officers starting to move. I have to run, but my feet are frozen! Everything is happening so fast, and now it's spiraling out of control. I look at the officers approaching where I am. I'm so scared right now I can't think. They are holding something, but it's not a gun, at least not a regular one. Crap, they're getting ready to fire tear gas at everyone! I need to warn everyone, but how can they hear me over all this noise? I look around and see a lamppost on the side of a street corner. As scared as I am, I manage to get my legs moving and run as fast as I can to the pole. With my legs shaking like a newborn deer, I climb up as high as I can and open my mouth. I want to say something profound, but the only thing I can manage is, "Hurry and run! They have tear gas!"

As soon as the words leave my mouth, the crowd begins to panic. People start running in different directions without looking where they're going. Off in the distance, people are covering their faces and putting goggles on. I guess they were prepared for this, but the majority of the people are not. I look up and see gas cans flying in the air. They land in the middle of the crowd and people begin to scatter. I slide myself down off the pole and immediately cover my mouth and close my eyes. What good that did. My eyes are hurting and I can't breathe. People are running past me, screaming and pushing. First, there's a loud bang, then a sharp pain in the back of my head. Then, blackness…

CHAPTER FOURTEEN

Bang! Is someone screaming? Sirens… What's happening around me? Oh, that's right, I got hit in the head. To my surprise, I wake to find myself face down on the asphalt. The ground is cold, my ears are ringing, and my eyes can't focus. What is happening? I try blinking my eyes to get them to focus. The first time didn't work, so I try again. Finally, I can see what's going on around me. The street is dark except for floodlights and car headlights. People are running everywhere, yelling at the police and each other. I slowly, gingerly stand up and find myself in the middle of everything.

Some protesters are fighting back, but they are outmatched by the officers. Is this how the protest was supposed to go? I can hear some chanting in the distance, but I can't see anything. I look to my left, but all I see is smoke. I begin to cough; my throat is scratchy from the smoke I'm inhaling. This smoke is choking me. I need to get out of here. Where is my car? I can't see anything!

Right when I say that, I look to my right and notice police officers rounding people up and putting them in a van. Oh no, what am going to do? The problems standing in the way of social justice are so much bigger than me. It's so much bigger than all of us! I can't handle this! I'm freaking out! This is the result of yelling and screaming at cops? *This is too much!* I don't know if it's my emotions or the gas, but tears stream down my face. How could I believe this is where I needed to be? I don't know where I am or where to go to get out of here!

Right when I was about to start running, a hand grabs my arm. I scream out, "No, let me go!" but it's too late. An officer has grabbed my arm and won't let go. I scream at the top of my lungs, "I didn't do anything! Let me go!" I start to struggle to try and get away, but it's no use. The officer's grip on me is too strong, and with each attempt at freedom, the grip tightens. "What are you doing?! Let go!"

"Calm down, Kiara!" a familiar voice says sternly. I look up and see someone I didn't expect. Officer Reeves?!

CHAPTER FIFTEEN

"Officer Reeves, I don't know what is happening. I don't know where to go."

"It's okay, I'm going to help you," she says calmly. Officer Reeves carefully pulls me to her side and leads me to a side street away from the other officers. She looks just as scared as I am, and neither of us knows what's going to happen next. The people are starting to regroup and the officers are continuing to move forward. This can get ugly fast. Officer Reeves looks at me and asks, "Where did you park?"

Dazed and confused, I try to reply. "Park?"

"Yes, you need to leave now!" she shouts. She's right, I have to pull myself together. This protest is a mess. I can't believe I wanted to go to something like this. They're not even voicing what they want; they're just yelling what they've lost.

The cops can't even hear them. They can't see them as a community this way either. The community meeting at Kat's house, that is where the people could be heard. Suddenly, I feel my body begin to shake.

"Kiara, snap out of it! Where… Where did you park?!" Officer Reeves shouts.

"Oh, sorry. I parked down the side road where the media was standing." My voice is shaking and my legs are heavy, but Officer Reeves drags me in the direction of the street corner where the media was at, but no one is there now. I'm not surprised; all the action is behind us and down the road. It looks like we're going to make it down the street when I hear voices behind us.

"Look, that officer is taking someone away! HELP HER!"

I turn around and a group of protesters are running toward us. My heart begins to pound as I see them holding bats and rocks. What do I do? I don't want Officer Reeves to get hurt. She was sneaking me away because she didn't want me to get hurt. Before I can finish my thought, I find myself standing in front of Officer Reeves with my hands out.

"Leave her alone!" I say with as much courage as I can muster. Shouting, I continue trying to convince them to stop. "You have to stop, she is helping me!" The group freezes with confused looks on their faces. I don't think they realize what they're doing. "Look, just go back to the protest or go home! This night isn't accomplishing anything!"

One of the protesters steps forward. "If you can say that, then you don't belong here! This may have gotten a little messier than we planned, but we're accomplishing a lot here tonight. Look at all the media coverage we're getting. This riot will be on all the news stations for weeks and that will force the world to see what's going on here in Georgia."

"What is your name?" Officer Reeves says.

"My name is Ezekiel, and there is nothing you can say to convince me you are on our side. We don't need you cops to police our community, we can do it ourselves. Hey girl, take your cop friend and go home yourself! We don't need naïve people who don't understand what's going on around here." After that, he and the group turned around and left.

I didn't realize there was another point to all this, but I do know that this kind of protesting isn't for me. I was so sure violent protesting would help me vent my frustration, but I was wrong. I was so happy participating in those other protests. I was meeting like-minded people and talking about the issues while having fun. That kind of protesting was no less productive of a demonstration, and at least there, no one was getting arrested. This kind of protest may be okay for Ezekiel, but it's not for me.

I snap myself back from my thoughts and look at Officer Reeves. "Officer Reeves, are you going to be okay?" I say with a smile.

"Yes, I'll be fine," she says back, but she's not smiling. "I have to get back and help the other officers. I just wanted to make sure you got out okay. Look, Kiara, you need to realize that even though protests like this get media attention, they also do more harm than good. So many people are going to jail or the hospital tonight. It's not worth it."

With a confident look on my face, I explain why I disagree with her. "I don't know if you're right about that, Officer Reeves. Yes, it's a shame people are getting hurt and arrested, but these people are out here because they are willing to sacrifice their freedom to be heard. I admit this type of protest isn't for me, but I *do* understand why it is for other people. They need to know their voices count for something, and right or wrong, they are being heard tonight. I don't expect you to understand, but I do expect you to acknowledge their sacrifice."

Officer Reeves stands in shock at what I just said. "I do understand going to the extreme for what you believe in, but can you truly believe that a night like this will bring progress? All

I see are good people lashing out in anger. When people see that on the news, they're not going to sympathize with your cause. They are going to want to lash out with their own anger. Violence only brings more violence! You have to see that!"

"What I see are people desperate for change and tired of no one listening to their cries for help! You heard Ezekiel, they are so fed up with the police, they would rather police themselves! I know your job is hard and mostly thankless, but you only need to be afraid of the bad guys. Black people have to be afraid of everyone, because we never know who is with us or against us! It's a paralyzing fear that stops us from applying for jobs or attending a school. You have no idea what that kind of life is like!"

"You're right, Kiara, I don't know what that's like." Officer Reeves lets out a loud, heavy sigh and moves toward me. Wait, what is she doing? Before I can move away, Officer Reeves grabs me one more time. This time, it isn't to save me from an angry crowd. She wraps her arms around me and gives me a hug. It is a big hug, like what you would get from your mom or your favorite aunt. "Sorry for not asking first, but you look like you really need this."

She's right. I hadn't realized it, but I had started crying again. It's funny, as we stand in the middle of a side street, it hits me. All this time, I wanted the cops to see and hear me. Now I'm here with Officer Reeves, a cop who hears me, feels my pain, and wants to work to make things better. Not just for me, but for the black community as a whole. I did it. I've accomplished my goal. I did a little yelling, but not in anger. It was in the pursuit of mutual understanding.

As my tears dry up, Officer Reeves releases me from her mommy hug and steps back. "You should get going before the roads close. I have to get back and help clear the streets."

"Okay, thank you for helping me. Be careful, Officer Reeves," I say, my voice still shaking.

Officer Reeves begins to walk away, but before she passes me, she turns her head and says, "I'm glad protests like this aren't your style,

Kiara. If you still want to express yourself tonight, there is a candlelight vigil in Brunswick. Why don't you go there?" Smiling under her mask, she walks back into the chaos and disappears around the corner.

CHAPTER SIXTEEN

After getting into my car, I start it up with nothing but home on my mind. If I go in the opposite direction, maybe I can get out of here. I can still hear the riot happening behind me. The sounds of shouting and sirens become fainter and fainter as I drive further and further away from the city. I still can't believe how intense that scene was. I was completely unprepared for an encounter like that. I wonder if Officer Reeves is okay. I don't like the police that much, but she was really nice. She stood with me and didn't try to take over the situation. She could have arrested me, but instead, she helped me get away. She didn't have to help me, and I definitely didn't give her reason to. Then she went back to that madness to stand with the other officers. What a crazy scene that was. Then she tried to help me salvage the night with a different demonstration. What was that demonstration she was talking about? Oh right, a candlelight vigil. But do I really want to do anything else tonight? I'm exhausted, and my mind is mush from all that chaos.

Wow, I'm tired, and I would love a bath right now. Not to mention, I think I have a knot growing on the back of my head. I feel back there, and sure enough, a small knot is behind my right ear. I don't think I need a hospital. It doesn't hurt much, but an ice pack wouldn't hurt.

I've been driving for about twenty minutes, and I don't know where I am. There are a lot of cars parked ahead of me. What's going on here? I park my car and slowly get out to see what is happening in front of me. I move closer and see people gathered in a tight group of about 25 people. Everyone is holding candles and hugging. Some are crying and talking amongst themselves, trying to adjust their masks to keep them in place. Is this the candlelight vigil Officer Reeves was talking about? I don't know how I got here, but this is a beautiful scene. I quietly move in closer so I can hear, but not be noticed. I don't want to interrupt what's happening, I just want to blend in quietly. A man notices me and walks toward me. Oh no, I didn't want this, not after what I just went through. I only want to be a part of a peaceful demonstration.

This is exactly what I need to calm my nerves and ease my heart. Everyone here is quietly remembering their lost loved ones, or consoling those who have lost loved ones. I don't want to draw any attention to myself by being noticed by anyone. I look down at the ground in hopes the man will take a hint and pass me by, but it's not long before I'm looking at a pair of shoes. Butterflies fill my stomach as I look up and begin to smile. "Hello, Simon."

"It's good to see ya found your way here, Kiara. Ya look like you've had a hard time gettin' here, though." Simon's face looks so gentle.

He must see the pain I'm feeling right now. It's hard, but look Simon right in the eye.

"I must look how I feel. I found that riot I was looking for, and it was exactly how you described it. I can still hear the screaming and shouting in my ears. I couldn't stay there, so with some help from an officer, I left and found my way here."

"I had a feelin' ya'd have to see it to believe it," Simon says with a nod.

"Well, I did see it, and I hope I never see it again. The people there were there for a reason, but I don't want to express myself that way. Do you understand, Simon?"

"Oh, I understand alright. That's why I'm glad ya here. These people are tryin' to overcome their grief with da comfort of God. You can do da same, Kiara."

"Yeah, I think I'll do that, Simon. I want to feel comforted and safe right now, and just standing amongst them has already made me feel much better."

I have met some amazing people today and seen some amazing things, but I believe I have finally found where I belong. I look around and see rows of people holding candles and each other. In this moment, I can feel the stress of the day melt out of my shoulders. I notice everyone is quieting down. Simon gives me a reassuring look and turns to face the inner circle.

There's a black man in the middle of the crowed holding a microphone in one hand and a Bible in the other. He holds the microphone up to his mouth and begins to speak. "Thank you, everyone, for coming tonight. Right now, there's a riot going on across town where people are damaging property and getting arrested. That is their way, but this is our way." Multiple *amens* ring out. "Let's say a prayer for their safety and the officers' safety. Lord, we gather here tonight to honor you and to ask you to protect our brothers and sisters who are fighting for what they believe in. Guide them and give them the strength needed to go the distance in this struggle for equality. Let no harm come to them or the ones sent to oppose them. Bless the officers, Lord! Give them your wisdom and let them feel your presence when they're on the job and among the people in the community they serve. Thank you, Lord Jesus. Amen." More *amens* rings out as the people become emotional from the man's prayer. I have tried to move away from this type of protesting, God's way of protesting, but it is futile. I truly feel he has been leading me here the whole time. I can't believe I didn't see it sooner, but I'm glad I'm here now.

Simon looks at me, holds out his hand and says, "Feel likc holdin' this old man's hand?" I smile and take his hand for a moment of silence. Exhaling, I blow away my fear and anger I brought with me to Georgia. I know the fight isn't over, but I'll find another way to fight. One that doesn't cause more suffering and pain. I can do so much more than yell at officers. I can use my talents to make a difference in my own way. A tear rolls down my cheek as a woman hands me a candle. I smile and say, "Thank you, sister."

CHAPTER SEVENTEEN

"Hey Kiara, are you finished with those documents yet?"

"Oh sure Melanie, and I remembered to number the pages this time."

"Oh, that's great! You have really become part of the team!"

"Thank you!" It's been two months since that eventful day in Georgia. I still can't believe I made it through that night in one piece. God is truly looking out for me. I met some amazing people that night and I'm trying to put what I learned to good use. I'm working for an organization trying to get racial equality legislature passed this coming senate hearing. The work I do for the Community Freedom Corp is hard, and maneuvering through all the political red tape is annoying, but I feel like I can make a difference here. This is how I'm going to protest social inequality.

"Kiara," a voice says from behind me. "Hey girl, stop spacing out. We have a speech to write."

"Sorry Kimra, I was just thinking about how I got here. It really has been an amazing journey," I say, smiling.

"Well, maybe you can tell me about it sometime. But for now, we have a lot of work to do. You know Allen, the organization's representative, has a hard time articulating his words, so we have to get this speech done by tomorrow or he's not going to make a very good impression."

"Okay, Kimra," I say with confidence. "Let's get started with his responses to questions, and then we can work on the opening of the speech."

Kimra looks at me with excitement in her eyes and says, "Okay, that sounds great! I'm really glad you came to join us!"

I smile back with a grateful look on my face. "I am too! Working here has truly given my life purpose. I have learned a lot about constructing new laws and getting them on the voting table. I believe I'm going to make a real difference here."

Kimra looks up; her eyes are so bright it's blinding. "I'm so glad you said that, Kiara, because I feel the same way as you. I believe I can make a real difference here as well. So, let's do our best, okay!"

"You got it, Kimra!"

We work into the night with not many breaks, but our dedication pays off. "This isn't bad, Kimra," I say with a smile.

"Yeah, Allen will have to review it and probably make a few tweaks to personalize it, but I like it," she says. "Especially the part about supporting a community over-watch committee."

"Yeah, that way, the number of citizen deaths by police can be monitored more closely," I say in agreement. Allen will need to make sure he focuses on that topic when he speaks, so the other State Senators will know how important it is.

While we're discussing the speech, I catch Melanie as she tries to leave for the day. "Hello Melanie, are you done for the day?"

"Yes, I finished my preparations for tomorrow. Have you two finished writing the speech for Allen yet?"

Kimra speaks up with a smile. "Oh yes, we just finished, and we believe it will go over well with the State Senate."

"That's great, ladies! This project has definitely been a group effort. I know Allen will be pleased with all of us. Especially if the Community Freedom Bill passes. That bill is a blueprint for giving people more say in what happens in their communities." I love seeing how determined and dedicated Melanie is to this project. She's been working on it longer than me or Kimra. In the beginning, it was only her and Allen. Now, they have a whole team working with them, and I am so proud to be a part of it.

Yawning, Melanie begins to move closer to the door. "Well, ladies, I'm heading home. Don't stay too long, okay?"

"Oh, we're not. Goodnight, Melanie," I say as she walks out.

"Yeah, goodnight!" Kimra yells a little too late. Melanie is already gone. Wow, she must have been really tired.

"So, can we call it a night?" I ask, completely exhausted. "We will have to be at the State Senate office bright and early tomorrow for the meeting."

Kimra looks at me with a yawn. "Okay, I guess that's enough for today. Why don't you meet me at the Senate office in the morning? I'll hand this to the representative tonight before I go home, so he can review it."

"Okay, that sounds great. Goodnight, Kimra."

"Goodnight, Kiara."

On my way home, I think about all I've done to get me where I am now. From my trip to Georgia and going from protest to protest only to realize violence isn't the answer for me, to looking inside and finding the way I want to bring about social change. The decision to join the Community Freedom Corp was an easy one. I'm glad an organization exists where I can use my talents to bring about positive change in my community. If it hadn't been for that night of chaos and confusion, I'd never have known I was capable of being part of something bigger than me. This is the feeling I was looking for while I was in Georgia. To think, all I had to do was look in my community newspaper to find it. Today it's writing speeches, tomorrow, who knows? But I do know that whatever I'm doing, I'll do it in a positive way with God by my side. That is my way and my path.

Acknowledgement

Thank you to Eloise Meneses, PhD. for always encouraging me to write at the best of my ability. I would not have had the courage to write this book without your confidence in my potential.